HOW TO REMOVE
MOVIE PROJECTOR FROM BOOK

Cut off plastic tie and discard. Hold on to
handle and lift projector straight out of base.
To store projector, simply snap back into the base.

HOW TO USE THIS PROJECTOR

- Pick a clear space on a light-colored wall or ceiling three to five feet away.
- The biggest image can be seen when the projector is five feet from the wall or ceiling.
- Use Disk 3 to begin. Change disks as indicated in the story.
- Slide the picture disk into the slot in the top of the projector as shown.
- Turn the disk to the right as you read through the story. The numbers next to the text correspond to the numbers on the projected images. Use the focusing ring to focus the pictures.

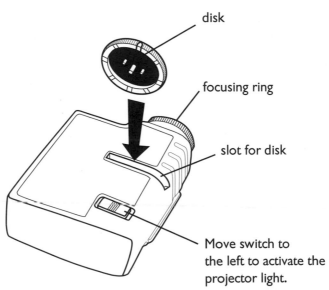

disk

focusing ring

slot for disk

Move switch to
the left to activate the
projector light.

PUPS' JUNGLE TROUBLE

adapted by MacKenzie Buckley

studio fun

A READER'S DIGEST COMPANY

White Plains, New York • Montréal, Québec • Bath, United Kingdom

One hot summer day, Ryder took the PAW Patrol pups on a road trip to the jungle to visit their friend Carlos. The

Disk 3
①

pups howled with excitement.

When the PAW Patroller stopped, the pups
hurried out and ran to greet Carlos. Marshall
jumped up and licked their friend's face.
"Hehe, that tickles!" laughed Carlos.

Ryder and the pups looked around the lush, green jungle surrounding them.

"What an amazing place to live!" said Ryder.

Marshall took off to explore. He climbed what he thought was a thick, green vine.

Suddenly, Mandy the monkey leaped in to join the group.

"Can I get a picture?"
Ryder asked the monkey.
But before he could tell
her to say "bananas,"
Mandy grabbed Ryder's
new PupPad and took off.

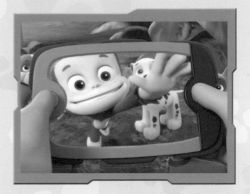

"Hey, wait," Ryder
called. "I need that back!"
It was too late. Mandy
had disappeared into
the jungle.

Ryder and Carlos raced back to the PAW Patroller. From there, Ryder was able to call the pups. They all hurried back to meet with Ryder.

"By using the PupPad's tracking device, we located Mandy," he said. "Looks like she's headed out of the jungle and into the hills."

"Uh-oh," said Carlos. "That's where the ancient temple ruins are. They're cursed!"

③

"Skye, I need you to use your helicopter to try to find Mandy from the sky," said Ryder.

"This puppy's gotta fly!" said Skye as she took to her copter.

"Chase," Ryder continued, "I need you and your superspy infrared goggles to track Mandy."

"Superspy Chase is on the case!" said Chase, who sped out on his spy truck.

Carlos hitched a ride on Ryder's ATV.

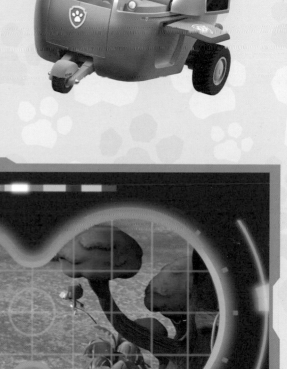

④ From her vantage point in the air, Skye spotted Mandy swinging through the trees.

"Ryder, Mandy and your PupPad arc headed toward the ruins," she radioed.

5984.110 6083.450

The team sped to the ruins. As they neared the ancient temple, they saw Mandy!

Mandy was at the top
of the stone door.
She smiled and then
disappeared inside.

Disk 4
1

"You guys wait
here—I'll go after her,"
said Ryder.

But Chase refused
to let Ryder go into the
ancient temple alone.

The ruins were pitch-black. Chase beamed his light so he, Ryder, and Carlos could get a good look around. Chase saw Mandy with Ryder's PupPad, but then she scampered off.

"Whoa! This place is so cool," said Ryder.

"And dangerous," warned Carlos. "The legend says if you take the necklace off the statue of the Monkey Queen, the temple will fall down."

"Awesome," yelped Chase.

"Look! There's Mandy," said Ryder. Chase pulled out his zip line and sped across it. "Betcha can't do this!" he taunted Mandy.

Mandy set down the PupPad and zip-lined down a vine. Ryder ran over and grabbed his PupPad. "Nice move, Chase!" he called.

But then they saw Mandy run over to the statue with the necklace. She grabbed it, and the ruins began to rumble.

"Oh, no!" shouted Carlos. "The curse!"

Disk 5

"Let's get out of here," Ryder yelled. The trio ran for the closing door, but outside, a huge boulder rolled in front of it before they could escape.

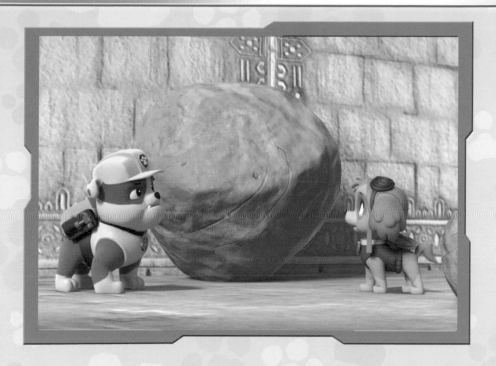

Ryder radioed Skye. "Think you can get us out?" he asked.

"Rubble will use his jackhammer to break apart the boulder so you can get through," said Skye.

②

"I'm on my way!" said Rubble, who sped from the PAW Patroller to the ruins.

While Rubble worked outside, inside Mandy dropped the necklace. Ryder hurried to place it back on the statue. The rumbling stopped just as Rubble finished clearing the boulder.

"Thanks for getting us out, pups," said Carlos.

"I knew all I'd have to do is yelp for help!" said Ryder.

BATTERY INFORMATION

To remove or insert replaceable batteries, remove the safety screw from battery compartment door. Lift and remove door. Take out and safely dispose of old batteries. Follow polarity diagram inside battery compartment to insert three new batteries of any of the following types: AG13 or equivalent. Alkaline batteries are recommended. Put battery compartment door back and secure safety screw. Do not use excess force or an improper type or size screwdriver.

GENERAL SAFETY AND CARE

- Non-rechargeable batteries are not to be recharged.
- Different types of batteries or new and used batteries are not to be mixed.
- Batteries are to be inserted with the correct polarity.
- Exhausted batteries are to be removed from the toy.
- The supply terminals are not to be short-circuited.
- Do not mix old and new batteries.

- Do not mix alkaline, standard (carbon-zinc), or rechargeable (nickel-cadmium) batteries.
- Prevent the book and unit from getting wet and avoid exposure to excessively hot or cold temperatures.
- Rechargeable batteries are only to be charged under adult supervision.
- Rechargeable batteries are to be removed from the toy before being charged.
- Remove batteries when not in use or discharged.

CAUTION

To ensure proper safety and operation, battery replacement must always be done by an adult. Never let a child use this product unless battery door is secure. Batteries are small objects and could be ingested. Keep all batteries away from small children and immediately dispose of any used batteries safely. Projector is not a viewer. Do not look into the lens when light is on.

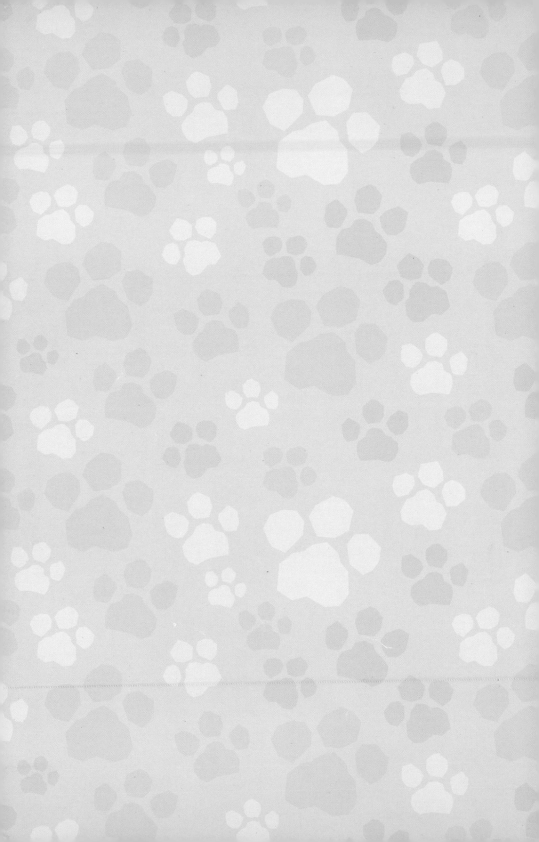